Written by Diane Wright Landolf
Illustrated by Mark Gravas and Suzanne White

 A GOLDEN BOOK • NEW YORK

As the head Easter Bunny in April Valley, Peter Cottontail was very busy. It was his job to make sure everything was ready in time for Easter.

Peter's son, Junior, was supposed to help—but Junior was more interested in working on his inventions.

"I'm going to make bunny history!" Junior said. He wanted to be just as famous as his father.

Peter wanted to teach Junior to be responsible. So he gave his son the important job of cleaning the magical Clock of Spring— one of the four clocks that controlled the seasons.

Junior took the key to the clock, planning to show Peter just how responsible he could be. But first, maybe there was a little time to tweak his latest invention, the Super-Charged Easter Basket Speed Shooter. . . .

Meanwhile, far away in her ice castle, Jackie Frost was brooding. She dreaded the coming of warm weather to melt all her beautiful ice sculptures. "I wish there were no such thing as spring!" she said.

"Perhaps I can help," said a stranger. It was Peter Cottontail's old enemy, Irontail! A long time ago, Peter and Irontail had competed for the job of head Easter Bunny. Peter won, and now Irontail wanted revenge. So he came up with a plan that would make winter last forever. There would never be an Easter!

Irontail, Jackie Frost, and her penguin henchmen headed to April Valley. Irontail put a fluffy bunny tail over his iron one so nobody would recognize him. Then he pretended to be interested in Junior's invention.

Meanwhile, Jackie and her gang sneaked into the clock through the back door. They climbed inside and stole the clock's magic charm, the Spring of Spring!

Just then, music started playing in the town square. The big Calendar Day celebration was about to begin, and Junior didn't want to miss it. Irontail volunteered to finish cleaning the clock. Junior accepted his offer—and even gave him the key.

Once Junior was out of sight, Jackie tossed the Spring of Spring to Irontail. Then the evil rabbit threw the key away and laughed as they sped off in Jackie's ice car.

Down in the town square, a crowd had gathered for the Calendar Day ceremony. Peter Cottontail stood in front of a calendar with his rabbit assistant, Elroy, and his caterpillar friend, Antoine.

"Welcome, friends!" he said. "Let's say goodbye to March and hello to April!"

The crowd cheered. Peter reached for the March 31 page on the calendar and flipped it over. The next page read March 32! But there was no such thing as March 32! Was it possible that April wasn't coming?

Junior ran to the Clock of Spring in a panic. The clock was completely frozen. The young bunny knew it was his fault. He had let everyone down. He left April Valley, determined to track down the thieves who had stolen the Spring of Spring.

Junior ran toward Summer Hill. If he could find the Clock of Summer, maybe he could catch the thieves before they stopped summer, too.

On his way, Junior met Flutter, a bird who wasn't very good at flying. Junior explained what had happened in April Valley, and Flutter agreed to lead him to the Clock of Summer.

But when they reached Summer Hill, it was too late—the Clock of Summer was already frozen!

The friends then ran to Fall Falls, where they met a helpful mouse named Munch. She quickly took them to the Clock of Fall.

Jackie and Irontail were already there.

"The Spring of Spring, the Sun of Summer, and the Leaf of Fall," said Irontail, juggling the three charms. "You know what this means? The seasons have stopped changing, and all that remains . . . is *winter*."

Just then, *whack!* Dozens of acorns came hurtling toward Jackie and Irontail. It was Junior and his friends! Irontail dropped the charms, and Flutter and Munch rushed to grab them. Unfortunately, Irontail swiped them back again. Then he removed his fluffy tail.

"Irontail!" exclaimed Junior.

"Say hi to your father for me," Irontail said with an evil laugh as the villains took off.

Junior and his friends felt hopeless. What could they do now? They walked and walked until they found themselves in Colorland, where every color of the rainbow comes from. There they met Mr. Seymour S. Sassafras and told him all about Irontail and Jackie Frost.

"Why don't you use my Incredible Bust-Proof Bubble to help you?" Mr. Sassafras suggested.

The three friends quickly hopped in—but they didn't get very
far. Luckily, they met Wind, who blew them all the way to Jackie
Frost's castle of ice.

Junior, Flutter, and Munch crept inside the castle. There on the wall were the magic charms! Junior quickly grabbed the charms, but Irontail spotted him.

"Cottontail!" Irontail yelled as he chased them outside.

They ran until they reached the Clock of Winter. As Jackie snatched the magic charms, Junior sneaked into the clock. He grabbed the Icicle of Winter.

Instantly, the wind and snow stopped. It wasn't winter anymore—or any season!

"What is with this rabbit?" asked Jackie Frost.

"He's just like his father," said Irontail. Irontail and Jackie threatened to throw the charms into a nearby pit. But Junior wouldn't be stopped!

"Give us back those, and I'll give you back this," Junior bargained, dangling the Icicle of Winter over the edge.

Jackie and Irontail couldn't agree on what to do.
"This is all your fault!" Irontail snarled at Jackie.
"Don't turn on me now!" Jackie snapped.
They began to fight and suddenly slipped over
the edge of the pit—with the charms!

Flutter dove after them. "No!" cried Junior. He was sure the bird wouldn't make it.

Zoom! Flutter rocketed out of the pit with the Sun of Summer, the Leaf of Fall, and the precious Spring of Spring.

"Yahoo!" shouted Junior and Munch.

The three friends quickly returned all the charms to their proper clocks. As Junior closed the Clock of Spring, he found the key his father had given him. Junior picked it up, then headed to April Valley.

"Junior!" Peter cried as he hugged his son. Junior felt safe at last.
"Not so fast, Cottontail," someone shouted. It was Irontail!
Zap! Jackie blasted her ice crystals at Peter and Junior. Thinking quickly, Junior dove in front of his father and used the key from the Clock of Spring as a shield. The blast bounced off it—and Irontail and Jackie Frost were frozen!

"I'm so proud of you, Junior," Peter said to his son.
Spring was saved! And once again, thanks to a Cottontail,
Easter would be coming soon!

PUBLICATION INFORMATION

Canadian Cataloguing in Publication Data
Tivy, Patrick, 1945-
A portrait of Calgary
ISBN 1-55153-090-2
1. Calgary (Alta.)--Pictorial works. I. Title.
FC3697.37.T58 1995 971.23'3803'0222 C95-910302-3
F1079.5.C35T58 1995

Design	Stephen Hutchings
Text	Patrick Tivy
Electronic page layout	Alison Barr and Sandra Davis
Financial management	Laurie Smith

Made in Western Canada
Printed and bound in Western Canada
by Friesen Printers, Altona, Manitoba.

Altitude GreenTree Program
Altitude Publishing will plant in Canada
twice as many trees
as were used in the manufacturing
of this book.

Photographic credits
Al Harvey: 3
Stephen Hutchings: 30T left, 47T
Lyle Korytar: 1, 10T, 12, 13, 14-15, 19T, 22-23, 25, 28 (inset), 31 middle, 38-39, 46, 47B
Douglas Leighton: Front cover
Bill Marsh: Back cover inset, 20, 21, 40, 41
Dennis Schmidt: 42
George Webber: Back cover, 8 (inset), 18B, 29T, 30B, 34-35
Deidre Williams: 4-5, 5 (inset), 6, 7T, 7B, 8, 9T, 9B, 10B, 11, 11 (inset), 16, 17T, 17B, 18T, 19B, 24, 26T, 26B, 27, 28, 29B, 30T right, 30B, 31T, 31B, 36T, 36B, 37T, 37B, 38-39 (insets), 43 (all), 44, 45T, 45B, 48

Altitude Publishing Canada Ltd.
The Canadian Rockies
P.O. Box 1410, Canmore Alberta T0L 0M0

A Portrait of
CALGARY

Hot air balloons offer a grand view of city and countyside.
Calgary is the balloon capital of Canada

Contents

Introduction to Calgary 4
Spirit of the West 36
Gateway to the Mountains 47

Introduction to Calgary

No one will ever accuse Calgarians of being shy and bashful, not when it comes to telling the world about the unique charms of their city. When you come to Calgary, you soon know you've arrived at a special place. You're in the "Heart of the Canadian West." You've entered the "Gateway to the Rockies." You are also at the "Oil Capital of Canada," the "City of the Foothills," as well as the "Host City of the 1988 Olympic Winter Games." As if that weren't enough, when you go to the Calgary Stampede, you can see the "Greatest Outdoor Show on Earth."

But don't be misled by the superlatives. Beneath all the glitz of Calgary's Wild West reputation you'll discover that all the superlatives are true. Calgary just isn't like ordinary cities. No other city in Canada makes such a fuss about having fun. The biggest festivities take place during Stampede. That's when the entire city gets dressed up in genuine Western gear. Some folks spend a lot of money on fancy boots, shirts with snap buttons, and wide-brimmed hats. In Calgary, normally staid banks and insurance offices decorate their premises with bales of hay and wagon wheels. There's even dancing in the streets. Grown men and women shout, "Yahoo!" It could only happen in Calgary.

Calgary has been blessed by nature. The geographical location at the junction of the Bow and Elbow rivers is one of exceptional beauty. The glorious Rockies gleam in the distance. And between city and mountains is range after range of rolling foothills. The cloud-free skies give Calgarians plenty of opportunities to enjoy gazing at the grand views that surround the city. The weather experts report that Calgary gets precisely 2314.4 hours of full sunshine each year, which is more than anywhere else in the nation.

From time to time, a gentle haze may settle over the hills but generally the soft western breezes keep the air sparklingly clear. The mists that obscure the view don't last long here because of the city's altitude. At a height above sea level of around 1100 metres (roughly 3500 feet), Calgary is the highest major city in Canada. The clear view can play tricks on the unwary. Sometimes the Rockies stand out so clearly on the horizon that they look like they were just a short walk away.

Calgarians take full advantage of the mountain playgrounds all year long. There are plenty of areas for downhill and cross-country skiing in the winter. In summer the skis are put away and out come bicycles, hiking boots, golf shoes, or climbing gear. The magnificent athletic facilities built for the 1998 Olympics are kept in constant use. And throughout the city is a spectacular network of paved riverbank trails used for hiking and biking. Calgary is a city where personal fitness is a popular passion.

That same energetic "let's-do-it" attitude characterizes the Calgary business community. The oil and gas industry is the main driving engine. Calgary is the head office of the Canadian petroleum industry. Most of the oil wells and refineries are scattered elsewhere across western Canada. Calgary's oil workers are employed in high-rise office towers, not on oil rigs.

Ranching and farming are still important, but more and more Calgarians are taking an active role in other industries. Calgary companies are now sending shipments of everything from office furniture to specialty beers to cus-

Above *Oil fuels Calgary's economic engine*

tomers as far afield as California and Oklahoma. Electronic and computer companies are on the cutting edge.

More than one visitor has come to Calgary with the intention of staying just a day or two. Then they discover that there's more to see, more to do, more to enjoy, than they ever expected. Many end up staying the rest of their lives. Calgary does that to people. Calgarians want everyone to feel right at home here. So, if you're a tourist, why not stay an extra day?

Calgary has a strong heart. The downtown area is the most popular "people place" in the city. Other cities have suffered as major retail stores moved to suburban shopping malls and corporations moved their offices to industrial parks in the warehouse districts. Calgary has managed to maintain the downtown core, and even improve the facilities that bring life to city streets.

The civic centre is focused on the grand plazas around City Hall, a dramatic sandstone landmark topped with a historic clock. Attached to City Hall is the new Municipal Building, a great glass triangle designed to let sunshine splash down on the Municipal Plaza. Across the street is the Olympic Plaza, scene of the medal presentations during the 1988 Winter Games.

Within a few short blocks are some of the finest shopping areas in the city. Most of the retail shops are connected by the Plus-15 system. (Plus-15s are pedestrian bridges built across busy downtown streets; Calgary has more of them than anywhere else in the world.) As well, close by is Calgary's Chinatown, filled with exotic shops and wonderful restaurants. Presiding over the whole downtown area is the Calgary Tower, which has a restaurant, lounge and observation deck.

Opposite City Hall was built of sandstone from local quarries
Above Bronze horses are a reminder of ranching heritage
Bottom Olympic Plaza

Opposite Striking architectural design of the Municipal Building provides dazzling reflections of downtown core

Opposite Inset Outdoor stage at Olympic Plaza is a popular place for summer entertainment

Above The Brotherhood of Mankind, *the imposing sculptural grouping by Mario Armengol, is one of Calgary's best-loved landmarks*

Bottom The Calgary Chinese Cultural Centre is modelled after the Temple of Heaven in Beijing, China

Opposite On warm summer days balloons blossom like fat round flowers in the cloudless skies above Calgary

Above The Eau Claire Market is a year-round "people place" featuring Alberta's first IMAX theatre and a variety of shops and restaurants

Bottom Colorful banners and bright lights create a festive mood along Barclay Parade in the Eau Claire Market district

U p, up, and away! Almost every day there are a few hot air balloons drifting over Calgary in the morning or afternoon breezes. During Stampede Week, there are even balloon races. The contestants take off from the infield in front of the Grandstand at Stampede Park.

Children love the play areas around Prince's Island Park. The park is on the edge of the downtown core and is one of Calgary's greatest treasures. Wee kiddies can frolic in the wading pool near the Eau Claire Market or clamber up the swings and slides. And children of all ages (even the young-at-heart office workers from the nearby office towers) love to feed the ducks and geese in the lagoon that separates Prince's Island from the south bank of the Bow River.

Prince's Island is always busy. Office workers stretch out on the lawns to relax and eat their lunches. At noon the trails around the island are packed with joggers, cyclists, and slow strollers. The island has a strategic location in the city's extensive network of riverbank paths. Business executives in need of some brief intensive exercise will take a short run up one side of the Bow, cross the river on one of the many nearby bridges, and run back on the other side.

The ducks and geese in the lagoon enjoy themselves so much that many ignore the normal urge to migrate and so they stay all winter long. Often a beaver family will build a dam on the stream below the weir that controls the level of water in the lagoon. It's a remarkable sight to see a beaver building a dam in the very heart of a big city. The cuddly-looking creatures nibble away on tender poplar branches even while dozens of curious people watch from the riverbank paths. Nature is very close to Calgary's heart.

Opposite A windmill like the ones used by pioneer farmers and ranchers whirls in the gentle summer breeze at the Eau Claire children's playground
Above *Ducks and geese are a year-round attraction at the Prince's Island lagoon*

D o yourself a favor in Calgary and take a trip along the riverbank pathways. You'll see parts of the city that can't be appreciated any other way. Most of the paths are paved and all of them are wheelchair-friendly, so virtually everyone can enjoy them. The paths are also connected to recommended bicycle routes on quiet residential streets that lead to all sections of the city.

From the pathway along the North bank of the Bow you'll get an astonishing view of the downtown skyline. The grand kaleidoscopic photograph on this page was taken from the path near the Zoo, but similar views can be found all along the riverbanks.

The paths are busy, especially on the weekends. Along the busiest stretches the paths have been divided into two, with bikes on one and pedestrians on the other, so that accidents can be avoided. Even so, there are parts further up and down the river in which a walker is able to enjoy the path in solitude.

One of the finest areas is through the trees along the South bank of the Bow west of Crowchild Trail. There are sections there that seem a million miles from civilization—but only until some other nature lover comes along.

A small prairie town still lurks beneath the surface of the modern big city of Calgary. It's easy to see in the historic pioneer architecture along the Stephen Avenue Mall. Especially during Stampede, when the streets are filled with people wearing old-fashioned cowboy hats, it doesn't take much imagination to squint your eyes and see the city as it used to be 70 or 80 years ago.

That small-town atmosphere along the Mall is being helped by a restoration program to dress up the street. Antique-style lamp posts have been installed. Many old buildings that were getting run-down have been restored to their former grandeur, often at great expense. The policy has helped prevent deterioration in the downtown area.

Several historic buildings have been saved by attaching them to new office towers. In other cases, only the exterior walls were preserved. Construction crews demolished the interiors, then rebuilt the structure according to modern standards.

The same small-town atmosphere prevails on the Mall itself. Because cars are rarely allowed on the Mall, it is the street where friends meet before heading off to lunch. It's prime strolling territory and a great

Opposite Flags of all nations wave in the breeze above the Stephen Avenue Mall **Above** The Mall is the "happening place" in the downtown business district **Bottom** The mounted patrol of the Calgary Police is a familiar sight on city streets and pathway

17

The last few decades have brought a new sense of maturity and sophistication to Calgary's cultural community. Calgarians now have a symphony orchestra with a ever-lengthening list of Compact Discs to its credit. The city has two major professional theatre companies, as well as several amateur troupes.

The Glenbow Museum has one of Canada's largest art galleries (and also has extensive holdings of Native artifacts, as well as relics from the pioneer era). The University of Calgary began as a branch of the University of Alberta and now is established as one of Canada's leading institutions of higher learning. Similar achievements have been accomplished by the Southern Alberta Institute of Technology, Mount Royal College and the Alberta College of Art.

Even athletic facilities are built with cultural needs in mind. The Olympic Saddledome is often used for concerts by all sorts of musicians, from raucous rock stars to sensational operatic soloists.

Opposite Top Calgary's first public library now includes a popular art gallery Opposite Bottom Heritage Hall at the Southern Alberta Institute of Technology is a registered landmark building Above The Olympic Saddledome at Stampede Park is the home of the Calgary Flames hockey team Bottom Street performers amuse visitors and downtown office workers

Above *The Olympic Torch atop the Calgary Tower is lit for special events*
Opposite *Observation decks and restaurant at Calgary Tower provide spectacular viewpoint*

It's probably just as well that some of the star attractions at the Calgary Zoo aren't really alive. The massive beasts that ramble through the Zoo's Prehistoric Park are dead, and have been for at least 65 million years, which no doubt cuts down on the Zoo's feeding expenses. The Prehistoric Park is where Calgary's most distant past is brought back to life. It is the home of realistic-looking models of the great dinosaurs that used to live here when the Alberta foothills were a boggy swamp on the edge of an inland sea.

That period of prehistory is very important to modern-day Calgary, because it was the origin of today's oil and gas industry. Through a long progression of geological processes, the

fertile swamps and coral reefs were buried under tonnes of sediment, then raised up through the mechanics of mountain-building. Slowly, over the millennia, the verdant vegetation and the various forms of sea life were transformed into oil, gas and coal.

As well, a remarkable number of the dinosaurs and other animals that ate the vegetation (and each other) have been preserved in the sedimentary rocks of Alberta. The foremost showcase for the dinosaur discoveries is at the Royal Tyrrell Museum at Drumheller. However, the Zoo's Prehistoric Park does a wonderful job of presenting the dinosaur replicas in lifelike situations, surrounded by plants that are similar (or, in some cases, even identical) to the greenery that existed millions of years ago.

A gentle path winds through the Prehistoric Park, leading visitors through a display of unusual geological formations, including hoodoos, erosion arches, and even a volcano.

Opposite Dinosaurs like this Tyrannosuarus Rex rule the earth at the Zoo's Prehistoric Park
Above Realistic dinosaur models are placed in lifelike poses in the park landscape

Above Right Flamingos are kept in an enclosure made to resemble natural wetland habitat

Above Left The antics of the Sumatran orangutans are always entertaining

Bottom The Zoo takes part in international programs to help preserve endangered species like the African white rhinoceros

Opposite The Conservatory is the centrepiece of the well-tended horticultural gardens at the Zoo

Zoo, as a word, seems too short a name for it. There is so much happening there, so many wonderful things to see and do, that somehow it deserves a name as long as a giraffe's neck. So, at least once, let's call it by its proper name: The Calgary Zoo, Botanical Garden and Prehistoric Park. Whatever it's called, though, the Zoo is one of Calgary's greatest treasures.

The Zoo is many things. To children, it's the place to pet a sheep or goat. To gardening enthusiasts, it's the place to inhale the scent of exotic flowers, or watch a butterfly wink its wings as it settles on a blossom. There are lions and tigers and bears and elephants and snakes and strange birds and, and, and…well, there are animals from all over the world.

Perhaps even more importantly, the Zoo has joined with other leading zoos around the world in programs to preserve endangered species and habitats. One of the most successful programs involves the Zoo's lowland gorillas. In the wild, the gorillas are slowly disappearing because of poaching and the destruction of the African forests. Working with other zoos that have gorillas, the Calgary Zoo has launched a coordinated mating program designed to prevent inbreeding. As well, by loaning or borrowing gorillas with other zoos, it is possible to maintain a healthy social structure in the gorilla groups. Long gone are the days when single animals were penned up in small cages. Today the Zoo creates display areas that are as large and natural as possible.

Calgary's climate, with its cold winters and chilling winds, presents a challenge to local gardeners. The Botanic Gardens are an inspiration and show what can be accomplished with enterprise and effort. The Conservatory is especially popular in the winter months. It includes a cactus desert area, as well as sections devoted to rain forest plants, palms, and a flower-filled butterfly garden.

Opposite The Calgary Tower
stretches skyward over its
glass-clad base
Opposite inset The moon
seems to appear three times
over the Calgary Tower in
this photograph of down-
town Calgary
Above The S.S. Moyie is a
popular attraction at
Heritage Park
Bottom This frontiersman is
dressed in the outfit that was
popular in the early days of
the rugged Canadian west

Above Left Spruce Meadows presents the finest equestrian competitors from around the world

Above Right The Science Centre makes science fun and entertaining

Bottom At Heritage Park the sights, sounds and smells of Western history come alive

Opposite Top There's a whirlwind of excitement available for all ages at Calaway Park on the western outskirts of Calgary

Opposite Middle Face-painting always brings out the smiles

Opposite Bottom The Corkscrew is is one of Calaway Park's wildest attractions. The roller-coaster ride goes up very slowly but comes down super fast

There are wooden sidewalks at Heritage Park where it's possible to stroll through history back to the days of the pioneers. You can ride a steam train, visit a historic farm, and even buy a loaf of bread from the bakery. The Alberta Science Centre/ Centennial Planetarium takes science out of the laboratory and makes it fun. The planetarium shows the latest discoveries from outer space, while the science centre is devoted to a variety of exhibitions ranging from reconstructed dinosaurs to "virtual reality" computer installations.

Spruce Meadows is one of world's foremost centres for equestrian competitions. Three major events are held each year.

Calaway Park, just 10 km. west of Calgary on the Trans-Canada Highway, is Calgary's favorite amusement park. Each summer it turns into an oasis of excitement, crammed with clowns, breath-taking rides, and special events.

The most important thing in the Olympic Games is not to win but to take part, just as the most important thing in life is not the triumph but the struggle.

Standing tall and proud on the western edge of the city are the ski jump towers of Canada Olympic Park, scene of many medal events during the 1988 Olympic Winter Games. The park is the handiest place for Calgarians to learn the fine points of downhill and cross-country skiing. As well, there are facilities for bobsleigh, luge and freestyle skiing.

The tall 90 Metre Ski Jump Tower is open for public tours. The observation deck on top offers a spectacular view of the city to the east and the foothills and mountains to the west. At the top of the luge run is the Naturbahn Teahouse, which serves a tasty (and critically-acclaimed) brunch on Sunday mornings.

Calgarians love the great outdoors and have a strong tradition of achievement in all types of winter sports. The exceptional facilities at Canada Olympic Park are kept busy from early fall to late spring. Classes are available for all schoolchildren, guaranteeing that Calgary will continue to be the home of champions for generations to come. The facilities, built at a cost of $72 million by the federal government, are administered by the Canada Olympic Development Association.

Spirit of the West

The first Stampede in 1912 was supposed to be a final farewell to the cowboys, who were then regarded as being a dying breed. The Native tribes, too, were supposed to be relics of days gone by. Obviously, those 1912 Stampede organizers were just plumb wrong.

Today, both cowboys and Native people are stronger than ever. And far from being a once-only celebration, the Stampede has grown into Canada's most famous annual tribute to the Western Way of Life.

The Stampede attracts the very finest rodeo athletes and offers the top prize money of all rodeos on the continent. The Stampede takes over the entire city. Some areas downtown are closed to traffic so that the citizens can squaredance on the pavement. Native tribes in full regalia parade through the city streets. Colorful banners are set lampposts and traffic lights along all the major thoroughfares. The city never looks better than it does during Stampede.

Opposite Top Historic finery is dusted off for the annual Stampede Parade
Opposite Bottom Blue jeans and cowboy hats are essential parts of Stampede gear
Above Barrel racers ride for top prize money at the Stampede rodeo competitions
Bottom Cowboys come from as far away as Australia and Brazil to compete at the Stampede

Don't ever blink while you're watching the Stampede or you'll miss something. The action is incredibly fast. Even the best bareback and saddle-bronc riders have to work hard to stay on for the required eight seconds. The ride is much shorter for cowboys who can't hold on. The famed Rangeland Derby features races by loaded chuckwagons accompanied by cowboys riding alongside at full gallop.

Rodeo today has developed strong links with the business community. Big-name corporations have fallen in love with the clean-cut cowboy image and pay many thousands of dollars for sponsorships and Western-style advertising campaigns. Of course, the rodeo at the Calgary Stampede is also show business, but it's show business with manure on its fancy boots. Most of the rodeo athletes are genuine farmers and ranchers and the events they compete in are based on routine ranch chores.

Getting bucked off a horse or a rampaging bull does look like a tough way to make a living, however, and it seems a strange way to have fun. Yet there is plenty of fun (along with some bruises and generous cash rewards) for rodeo athletes. For them, it's all in a day's work.

The horses and cattle at the Stampede are the royalty of the animal kingdom. They're pampered like prize-winning pussy cats. Many have a working day that's over in eight seconds or less. There have been very few changes to rodeo competitions since the first Stampede in 1912. The major difference today is the array of rules and regulations—as well as the herds of judges, inspectors, and animal welfare officers—which govern what happens at the Stampede.

There are stringent rules for all rodeo sports. Infringements mean penalty points that can put a contestant out of the money. There's even a dress code. Anyone who ventures into the infield must be in full western garb, especially the wide-brimmed cowboy hat.

Rodeo gets in the blood and has become a tradition in many Alberta ranching families. The same surnames are the top of the prize lists year after year, generation after generation. Almost every young rodeo athlete has a cousin or a grandparent who used to rodeo. Rodeo competitors get together after the day's work is done. They share expenses and take turns driving the pickup truck to the next rodeo.

Many become friends for life.

Rodeo athletes come from all over the ranching world—from the U.S, Australia, and Brazil—to compete at Calgary. The Stampede is known internationally as the fat purse rodeo. No other rodeo, no state fair, nor any "frontier days" celebration anywhere can match the Stampede's largesse when it comes to Rodeo's Richest Hour.

During Rodeo's Richest Hour five cowboys are presented with trophies, belt buckles, championship rings, sponsorship bonuses, all topped off with Stampede Grand Prize cheques for $50,000 each. The magic Hour comes on the final Friday of the infield events. It's a moment of glory that young cowboys dream about, and that old cowboys remember forever. It just doesn't get any better.

Above Bull riders must hang on with only one hand. A successful ride will last for a complete eight seconds

Opposite There are more horses in the foothills country around Calgary than anywhere else in Canada. Horses used on ranches are bred for their strength, speed and endurance

Above Left The Western Saddle is built for hard work. The design provides comfort for riders who spend many hours on horseback

Above Right The cowboy's wide-brimmed hat keeps the sun out of his eyes and stops the rain from running down his neck The leather chaps protect his legs while riding through the scrub

Middle A cowboy's buckle does more than keep his belt fastened. An engraved silver buckle can be a trophy, a personal memento, and an advertisement of great accomplishments

Bottom Spurs, stirrups and boots all reflect the experience and personality of the individual cowboy

L ife on a ranch can be tough. Cattle don't work on a 9 to 5 shift, and neither do the men and women who tend them. In calving season, for instance, it simply doesn't matter what the clock says—there are chores to be done and someone has to do them. Ranchers often find themselves at the mercy of an unsympathetic marketplace. At the end of the year, there are many who feel they've done well if they just break even. But there's something about the cowboy way of life that provides a richer reward. For many, living close to the land makes it all worthwhile.

Opposite *The hardy wild prairie rose is the floral symbol of Alberta*
Above *Even on frosty spring mornings there is work to be done on a foothills ranch*
Bottom *They call Alberta "Big Sky Country." Some cowboys feel hemmed in and trapped when they go to town*

Above The snow-capped Rockies provide a
magnificent backdrop for the rolling
foothills to the west of Calgary
Opposite top Mount Kidd is one of the most
dramatic peaks in Kananaskis Country
Opposite bottom The glorious Rockies always seem
to be changing; there is something
new and beautiful about them every day